D1074672

THE GOBLIN
UNDER THE STAIRS

story by Mary Calhoun
pictures by Janet McCaffery

William Morrow & Company

Text copyright © 1967 by Mary Calhoun
Illustrations copyright © 1968 Janet McCaffery
all rights reserved
Published simultaneously in Canada
by George J. McLeod Limited, Toronto
Printed in the United States of America
Library of Congress Catalog Card Number
68-13001

Well, one time in the north of England
there was a hairy boggart who moved himself into a farmhouse.
The boggart was a kind of goblin-man.
He settled himself in a closet under the stairs.
And there he sat, all snug and warm for the winter.
Wasn't long, though, before a child found him.

The boy was bouncing a ball in the kitchen by the closet wall,
when he heard something rustling in there.
Was a knothole in the wall,
so the boy put his eye to the hole.
Whups, he saw a little man.
There was a little goblin-man covered with shaggy hair,
a-grinning and winking at him.
He was the boggart.
Well, the boy never knew
there was a boggart under the stairs.

He opened the closet door and looked.

No little man in there. Nothing but brooms in there.

The boy put his eye back to the peephole.

Sure enough, he could see the wee hairy creature.

Now everybody in Yorkshire, there in the north of England,

knew the way to see fairies was to look through a knothole.

For a hole points the eye to things unknown.

So the boy knew he had him a boggart in there.

The boggart was all frisking and grinning,

and what he liked was to play.

He waved for the boy to throw in his ball.

The boy did,

and the boggart hurled the ball back out the hole, roughlike.

The boy kept pushing his ball through the hole,

and the boggart kept shooting it back to him.

While they played,
the little shaggy man taught the boy
a song that went squeak, squeak, SQUEAK!
Pretty soon the farmer and his wife came along.
When the ball came flying out the hole,
the farmer said to his boy, "What you got in there?"
"A boggart," said the boy.
"He's a wee frisky man, and he's playing with me."
The wife put her eye to the knothole.
She saw a neat little man
with wide strong shoulders and smooth furry coat.
"Aye, he's a boggart!" said she.
"He's a good servant elf,
and he'll clean the kitchen for me."

The farmer put his eye to the hole.

He saw a wild hairy creature with wild glary eyes.

"He's a boggart!" said he.

"He's a house-plaguing goblin,

and he'll torment the life out of me."

Then, though the child cried,

the farmer told the boggart to go,

to get out of that house and never come back.

But that's not the end of it.

The boggart didn't go.

That night when the folks went to bed,

the boggart popped out through the hole.

And he was a house-plaguing goblin,

just as the farmer said.

Hopping on his short legs, waving his long arms,

he went twisty-spinning, twisty-spinning all around the room.

Then he fixed the place up, boggart fashion.

In the kitchen he threw the table on its back,
stamped out the fire, smashed the dishes on the floor,
all the time squeaking and grinning and twisty-spinning.
In the barn he scattered the hay all about,
tied knots in the rope, drove the cow off to the woods,
all the time squeaking and grinning and twisty-spinning.

All over the house the wild hairy creature
tromped in the halls and knocked on the walls.
He yelled and sang squeak, squeak, SQUEAK,
to wake everybody up.
Then he popped back through the hole,
curled up under the stairs, and went to sleep.

Next morning, oh lawk and oh my!
The goodwife found her kitchen turned topsy-turvy.
The farmer found his barn turned higgledy-piggledy,
and the cow was gone.
Even the boy's ball was gone.
"The boggart's still here!" cried the boy.
He ran to the knothole, and his ball shot out at him.
The boy laughed. The wife threw up her hands.
But the farmer, he stomped and roared and pulled his hair.
He vowed he'd get rid of that house-plaguing goblin.
First he tried to smoke the boggart
out from under the stairs.

He set a smudge pot in the closet,
locked the door, and plugged the knothole.
The family stood in the kitchen,
waiting for the boggart to disappear.
But the plug flew out of the hole.
Smoke poured out and swirled around the farmer's head.
And there in the smoke was the boggart's face, grinning.
The boy clapped his hands. "The boggart's still here!"

The farmer raged and beat the air

until the boggart-grin smoke wisped back through the hole.

Then, quick, the farmer tried to seal him up in there.

He got boards and nailed them over the hole and the door.

But those boards sailed off and rapped him on the nose.

On every board was the boggart's grin.

The boy danced with a boggart-grin board.

"The boggart's still here!" he said.

At last the farmer made a plan.

They'd pretend to move away, he whispered to his wife.

No boggart would stay when a house passed into new hands.

When they came back, the house-plaguing pest would be gone.

In a loud voice he said,

"That old hairy boggart is too much for us.

It's time to flit away.

We'll sell the place to a neighbor."

The farmer and his goodwife

gathered up everything in the house, tables and tubs and all.

Piled the furniture into a cart. Going to leave forever.

The boy, he cried and ran to the peephole for one last look.

"Good-bye," he said to the frisky man.

Then off down the road they went.

The wife drove the cow, the farmer led the cart,
and the boy rode on top of the household goods.
Before long they met a neighbor.
"What, are you moving today?" said the man.
And from a tub on the cart came a squeaky voice.

"Aye, neighbor, we're flitting today, you see."
It was the boggart, going right along with his folks.
Well, the farmer was that disgusted,
he turned the cart around and went back to the house.
There was no getting rid of the boggart, he saw.

But the boy clapped his hands, and the wife was glad, too.

She still hoped the boggart would be her servant elf.

The farmer gave up, let her have her way.

She was a good Yorkshire farmwife, and she knew what to do.

That night she swept the hearth.

In a corner by the fire she set out a bowl of fresh cream

and an oatcake spread with honey.

Then the folks went to bed.

When all was quiet, the boggart slipped out through the hole.

And he was a neat servant elf, just as the wife had said.

He sat on the hearth in his smooth fur coat,
and he lapped up the cream, and he ate up the honey cake.
Then he fixed the place up, boggart fashion.

Squeaking and grinning and twisty-spinning,
he washed the dishes and scrubbed the floor.
He cleaned the pots, and he churned the butter.

In the barn he milked the cow and gave her hay.

He cleared out the muck and threshed the grain.

Last, back to the house he went twisty-spinning,

and he tromped one loud *thump* that woke everybody up.

Because after all, he *was* a boggart.

Then he whisked through the hole and went to sleep.

In the morning, oh lawk and oh my!

The goodwife found her kitchen

sparkling like a new-washed window.

The farmer found his barn full of a day's work.

The boy peeked through the hole

and found the boggart still in there, winking at him.

That's the way it went, from that day on.

Every night the wife set out cream and a honey cake.

Every night the boggart worked for the farmer and his wife.

Every day he played with the boy at the hole.

Between times he squeaked in the halls
and pulled tricks on them all.
They never did see him, except through the hole.
Whenever they looked,

the farmer saw a wild hairy goblin,
the wife saw a neat servant elf,   the boy saw a wee frisky man.

That's how they saw the boggart under the stairs.
And for all I know, he's still in there.

AUTHOR'S NOTES

The boggart of Yorkshire and Lancashire lore in north England is more definitely a poltergeist than many of the European house elves. Folktales emphasize that he is a tormenting, tempestuous spirit, with fewer human characteristics than such elves as the Danish nisse and the Swedish tomten.

The pesty elf's trick of hiding in a cart to move with the family is a motif found in tales from other countries—Wales, Ireland, Germany, and Denmark —as well as England.

Also widespread is the idea that magical creatures may be seen through a hole. In Scotland a knothole is called an elfbore, and some believe that fairies and elves may be viewed through it. Tales of fairies seen through holes or entering through them are found in Germany and Denmark. In the latter country it is said that anyone who looks through a hole will see things he would not otherwise have known. And in the Mesa Verde cliff dwellings of southwestern Colorado in the United States, ceremonial kivas have small holes called sipapu. According to Indian belief, spirits from the underworld entered through them.

My primary sources for this story are: *English Folk and Fairy Tales*, by Joseph Jacobs, *Fairy Tradition in Britain*, by Lewis Spence, and *The Fairy Mythology* by Thomas Keightley.

The End